SH

Compiled and Illustrated
by
Patricia Machin

Webb & Bower
EXETER ENGLAND

First published in Great Britain 1985 by
Webb & Bower (Publishers) Limited
9 Colleton Crescent, Exeter, Devon EX2 4BY

Copyright © Webb & Bower (Publishers) Limited 1985

British Library Cataloguing in Publication Data
Shelley, Percy Bysshe
  Shelley.–(Webb & Bower pocket poets)
  I. Title II. Machin, Patricia
  821'.7 PR5403

  ISBN 0-86350-046-3

All rights reserved. No part of this publication may be
reproduced, stored in a retrieval system, or transmitted
in any form or by any means, electronic, mechanical,
photocopying recording or otherwise, without the prior
permission of the Copyright holders.

Typeset in Great Britain by P & M Typesetting Limited,
Exeter, Devon

Printed and bound in Hong Kong by Mandarin Offset
International Limited

Contents

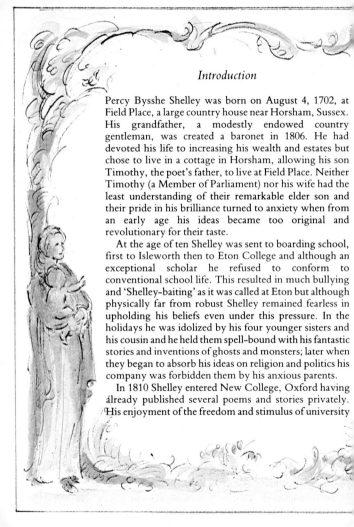

Introduction

Percy Bysshe Shelley was born on August 4, 1702, at Field Place, a large country house near Horsham, Sussex. His grandfather, a modestly endowed country gentleman, was created a baronet in 1806. He had devoted his life to increasing his wealth and estates but chose to live in a cottage in Horsham, allowing his son Timothy, the poet's father, to live at Field Place. Neither Timothy (a Member of Parliament) nor his wife had the least understanding of their remarkable elder son and their pride in his brilliance turned to anxiety when from an early age his ideas became too original and revolutionary for their taste.

At the age of ten Shelley was sent to boarding school, first to Isleworth then to Eton College and although an exceptional scholar he refused to conform to conventional school life. This resulted in much bullying and 'Shelley-baiting' as it was called at Eton but although physically far from robust Shelley remained fearless in upholding his beliefs even under this pressure. In the holidays he was idolized by his four younger sisters and his cousin and he held them spell-bound with his fantastic stories and inventions of ghosts and monsters; later when they began to absorb his ideas on religion and politics his company was forbidden them by his anxious parents.

In 1810 Shelley entered New College, Oxford having already published several poems and stories privately. His enjoyment of the freedom and stimulus of university

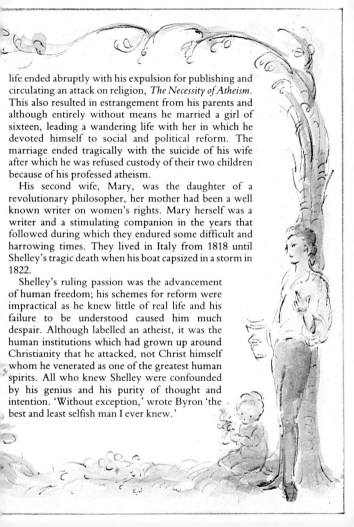

life ended abruptly with his expulsion for publishing and circulating an attack on religion, *The Necessity of Atheism*. This also resulted in estrangement from his parents and although entirely without means he married a girl of sixteen, leading a wandering life with her in which he devoted himself to social and political reform. The marriage ended tragically with the suicide of his wife after which he was refused custody of their two children because of his professed atheism.

His second wife, Mary, was the daughter of a revolutionary philosopher, her mother had been a well known writer on women's rights. Mary herself was a writer and a stimulating companion in the years that followed during which they endured some difficult and harrowing times. They lived in Italy from 1818 until Shelley's tragic death when his boat capsized in a storm in 1822.

Shelley's ruling passion was the advancement of human freedom; his schemes for reform were impractical as he knew little of real life and his failure to be understood caused him much despair. Although labelled an atheist, it was the human institutions which had grown up around Christianity that he attacked, not Christ himself whom he venerated as one of the greatest human spirits. All who knew Shelley were confounded by his genius and his purity of thought and intention. 'Without exception,' wrote Byron 'the best and least selfish man I ever knew.'

While the Shelleys were
at Pisa in 1820 they became
close friends of the Masons; they
visited Mrs Mason, an
enlightened and sympathetic
woman, every day for several
months. It is believed that this lady's
personality and her beautiful garden
contributed to this poem in which
Shelley casts himself as the sensitive
plant. When 'the lady, the wonder of
her kind' dies her coffin is borne
through the garden after which
death and corruption set in.
Only the first part of the poem
is illustrated here; Shelley's
descriptions of flowers are
astonishingly vivid and
beautiful.

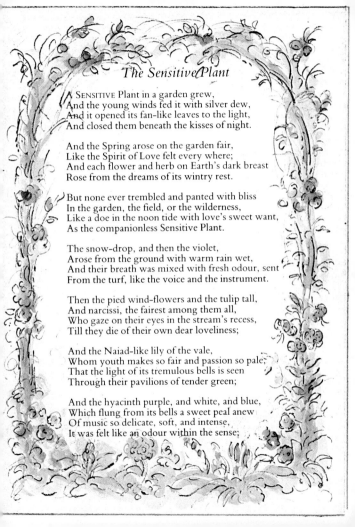

The Sensitive Plant

A SENSITIVE Plant in a garden grew,
And the young winds fed it with silver dew,
And it opened its fan-like leaves to the light,
And closed them beneath the kisses of night.

And the Spring arose on the garden fair,
Like the Spirit of Love felt every where;
And each flower and herb on Earth's dark breast
Rose from the dreams of its wintry rest.

But none ever trembled and panted with bliss
In the garden, the field, or the wilderness,
Like a doe in the noon tide with love's sweet want,
As the companionless Sensitive Plant.

The snow-drop, and then the violet,
Arose from the ground with warm rain wet,
And their breath was mixed with fresh odour, sent
From the turf, like the voice and the instrument.

Then the pied wind-flowers and the tulip tall,
And narcissi, the fairest among them all,
Who gaze on their eyes in the stream's recess,
Till they die of their own dear loveliness;

And the Naiad-like lily of the vale,
Whom youth makes so fair and passion so pale,
That the light of its tremulous bells is seen
Through their pavilions of tender green;

And the hyacinth purple, and white, and blue,
Which flung from its bells a sweet peal anew
Of music so delicate, soft, and intense,
It was felt like an odour within the sense;

And on the stream whose inconstant bosom
Was prankt under boughs of embowering blossom,
With golden and green light, slanting through
Their heaven of many a tangled hue.

Broad waterlilies lay tremulously,
And starry river-buds glimmered by,
And around them the soft stream did glide and dance
With a motion of sweet sound and radiance.

And the sinuous paths of lawn and of moss,
Which led through the garden along and across,
Some open at once to the sun and the breeze,
Some lost among bowers of blossoming trees,

Were all paved with daisies and delicate bells
As fair as the fabulous asphodels,
And flowrets which drooping as day drooped too
Fell into pavilions, white, purple, and blue,
To roof the glow-worm from the evening dew.

And from this undefiled Paradise
The flowers (as an infant's awakening eyes
Smile on its mother, whose singing sweet
Can first lull, and at last must awaken it,)

When Heaven's blithe winds had unfolded them,
As mine-lamps enkindle a hidden gem,
Shone smiling to Heaven, and every one
Shared joy in the light of the gentle sun;

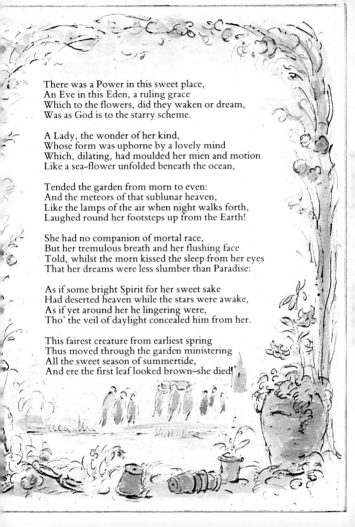

There was a Power in this sweet place,
An Eve in this Eden, a ruling grace
Which to the flowers, did they waken or dream,
Was as God is to the starry scheme.

A Lady, the wonder of her kind,
Whose form was upborne by a lovely mind
Which, dilating, had moulded her mien and motion
Like a sea-flower unfolded beneath the ocean,

Tended the garden from morn to even:
And the meteors of that sublunar heaven,
Like the lamps of the air when night walks forth,
Laughed round her footsteps up from the Earth!

She had no companion of mortal race,
But her tremulous breath and her flushing face
Told, whilst the morn kissed the sleep from her eyes
That her dreams were less slumber than Paradise:

As if some bright Spirit for her sweet sake
Had deserted heaven while the stars were awake,
As if yet around her he lingering were,
Tho' the veil of daylight concealed him from her.

This fairest creature from earliest spring
Thus moved through the garden ministering
All the sweet season of summertide,
And ere the first leaf looked brown—she died!

Prometheus

This long poem, of which
only a few lines are illustrated
here, is considered Shelley's
greatest lyrical drama. Modell-
ed on the work of the Greek
poet Aeschylus, it portrays
Prometheus as the champion of
mankind, chained to a rock and
subjected to perpetual tor-
ture. Shelley's biographer, N I
White, accords the success of
this masterpiece to 'the steady
growth of an extraordinarily
fine mind' and adds 'the sudden
lyrical splendour is practically
unexplainable.'

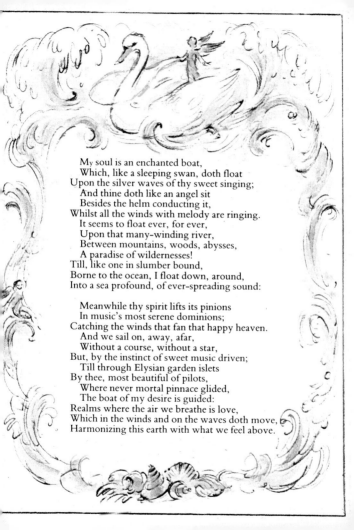

My soul is an enchanted boat,
   Which, like a sleeping swan, doth float
Upon the silver waves of thy sweet singing;
   And thine doth like an angel sit
   Besides the helm conducting it,
Whilst all the winds with melody are ringing.
   It seems to float ever, for ever,
   Upon that many-winding river,
   Between mountains, woods, abysses,
   A paradise of wildernesses!
Till, like one in slumber bound,
Borne to the ocean, I float down, around,
Into a sea profound, of ever-spreading sound:

   Meanwhile thy spirit lifts its pinions
   In music's most serene dominions;
Catching the winds that fan that happy heaven.
   And we sail on, away, afar,
   Without a course, without a star,
But, by the instinct of sweet music driven;
   Till through Elysian garden islets
   By thee, most beautiful of pilots,
   Where never mortal pinnace glided,
   The boat of my desire is guided:
Realms where the air we breathe is love,
Which in the winds and on the waves doth move,
Harmonizing this earth with what we feel above.

Shelley suffered periods of deep despondency when it seemed that all enjoyment of life had deserted him. To release his spirit from this prison of oppression, so that he could return again to the world of imagination in which he created his poems, required tremendous courage and tenacity resulting in some of the world's finest poetry.

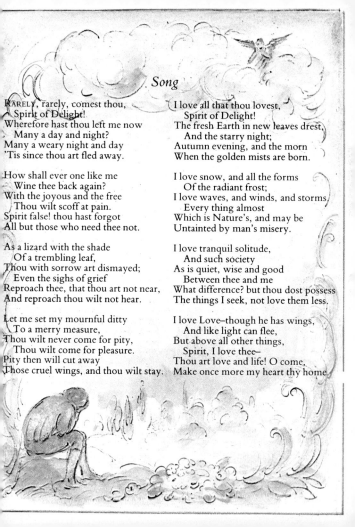

Song

RARELY, rarely, comest thou,
  Spirit of Delight!
Wherefore hast thou left me now
  Many a day and night?
Many a weary night and day
'Tis since thou art fled away.

How shall ever one like me
  Win thee back again?
With the joyous and the free
  Thou wilt scoff at pain.
Spirit false! thou hast forgot
All but those who need thee not.

As a lizard with the shade
  Of a trembling leaf,
Thou with sorrow art dismayed;
  Even the sighs of grief
Reproach thee, that thou art not near,
And reproach thou wilt not hear.

Let me set my mournful ditty
  To a merry measure,
Thou wilt never come for pity,
  Thou wilt come for pleasure.
Pity then will cut away
Those cruel wings, and thou wilt stay.

I love all that thou lovest,
  Spirit of Delight!
The fresh Earth in new leaves drest,
  And the starry night;
Autumn evening, and the morn
When the golden mists are born.

I love snow, and all the forms
  Of the radiant frost;
I love waves, and winds, and storms,
  Every thing almost
Which is Nature's, and may be
Untainted by man's misery.

I love tranquil solitude,
  And such society
As is quiet, wise and good
  Between thee and me
What difference? but thou dost possess
The things I seek, not love them less.

I love Love—though he has wings,
  And like light can flee,
But above all other things,
  Spirit, I love thee—
Thou art love and life! O come,
Make once more my heart thy home.

To Night

SWIFTLY walk over the western wave,
  Spirit of Night!
Out of the misty eastern cave,
Where, all the long and lone daylight,
Thou wovest dreams of joy and fear,
Which make thee terrible and dear, –
  Swift be thy flight!

Wrap thy form in a mantle grey,
  Star-inwrought!
Blind with thine hair the eyes of day;
Kiss her until she be wearied out,
Then wander o'er city, and sea, and land,
Touching all with thine opiate wand –
  Come, long sought!

When I arose and saw the dawn,
  I sighed for thee;
When light rode high, and the dew was gone,
And noon lay heavy on flower and tree,
And the weary Day turned to his rest,
Lingering like an unloved guest,
  I sighed for thee.

Thy brother Death came, and cried,
  Wouldst thou me?
Thy sweet child Sleep, the filmy-eyed,
Murmured like a noon-tide bee,
Shall I nestle near thy side?
Wouldst thou me? – And I replied,
  No, not thee!

Death will come when thou art dead,
  Soon, too soon –
Sleep will come when though art fled;
Of neither would I ask the boon
I ask thee, beloved Night –
Swift be thine approaching flight.
  Come soon, soon!

It has been suggested that some of the rhythmic power of Shelley's poems, which never fail to astonish the reader with their variety and originality, may stem from the poet's intense interest in music. This beautiful poem, written towards the end of his life, was published posthumously.

Autumn: A Dirge

THE warm sun is failing, the bleak wind is wailing,
The bare boughs are sighing, the pale flowers are dying,
    And the year
On the earth her death-bed, in a shroud of leaves dead,
    Is lying.
    Come, months, come away,
    From November to May,
    In your saddest array;
    Follow the bier
    Of the dead cold year,
-And like dim shadows watch by her sepulchre.

The chill rain is falling, the nipt worm is crawling,
The rivers are swelling, the thunder is knelling
    For the year;
The blithe swallows are flown, and the lizards each gone
    To his dwelling;
    Come, months, come away;
    Put on white, black, and grey;
    Let your light sisters play–
    Ye, follow the bier
    Of the dead cold year,
And make her grave green with tear on tear.

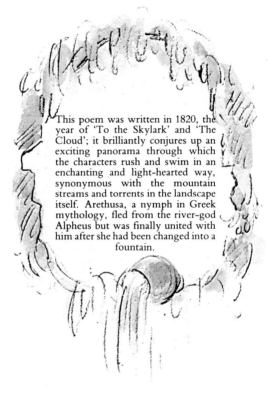

This poem was written in 1820, the year of 'To the Skylark' and 'The Cloud'; it brilliantly conjures up an exciting panorama through which the characters rush and swim in an enchanting and light-hearted way, synonymous with the mountain streams and torrents in the landscape itself. Arethusa, a nymph in Greek mythology, fled from the river-god Alpheus but was finally united with him after she had been changed into a fountain.

Arethusa

ARETHUSA arose
  From her couch of snows
In the Acroceraunian mountains,–
  From cloud and from crag,
  With many a jag,
Shepherding her bright fountains.
  She leapt down the rocks,
  With her rainbow locks
Streaming among the streams;–
  Her steps paved with green
  The downward ravine
Which slopes to the western gleams:
  And gliding and springing
  She went, ever singing,
In murmurs as soft as sleep;
  The Earth seemed to love her,
  And Heaven smiled above her,
As she lingered towards the deep.

Then Alpheus bold,
   On his glacier cold,
With his trident the mountains strook;
   And opened a chasm
   In the rocks;–with the spasm
All Erymanthus shook.
   And the black south wind
   It unsealed behind
The urns of the silent snow,
   And earthquake and thunder
   Did rend in sunder
The bars of the springs below:
   And the beard and the hair
   Of the river God were
Seen through the torrent's sweep,
   As he followed the light
   Of the fleet nymph's flight
To the brink of the Dorian deep.

   'Oh, save me! Oh, guide me!
   And bid the deep hide me,
For he grasps me now by the hair!'
   The loud Ocean heard,
   To its blue depth stirred,
And divided at her prayer;
   And under the water
   The Earth's white daughter
Fled like a sunny beam;
   Behind her descended
   Her billows, unblended
With the brackish Dorian stream:–
   Like a gloomy stain
   On the emerald main
Alpheus rushed behind,–
   As an eagle pursuing
   A dove to its ruin
Down the streams of the cloudy wind.

Under the bowers
Where the Ocean Powers
Sit on their pearled thrones,
Through the coral woods
Of the weltering floods,
Over heaps of unvalued stones;
Through the dim beams
Which amid the streams
Weave a net-work of coloured light;
And under the caves,
Where the shadowy waves
Are as green as the forest's night:—
Outspeeding the shark,
And the sword-fish dark,
Under the Ocean's foam,
And up through the rifts
Of the mountain clifts
They past to their Dorian home.

And now from their fountains
In Enna's mountains,
Down one vale where the morning basks,
Like friends once parted
Grown single-hearted,
They ply their watery tasks.
At sunrise they leap
From their cradles steep
In the cave of the shelving hill;
At noon-tide they flow
Through the woods below
And the meadows of Asphodel;
And at night they sleep
In the rocking deep
Beneath the Ortygian shore;—
Like spirits that lie
In the azure sky
When they love but live no more.

The Shelleys, with their baby
son born after William's death
the previous year, spent the
summer of 1820 at Bagna di
San Guiliano near Pisa. While
Mary continued with her own
writing, Shelley explored the
canal onto which the house
backed and its adjoining rivers
and countryside and wrote
some of his most brilliant
poems. The reader cannot fail
to be drawn into the dizzy
heights of the astonishing
cloud-scapes created by
Shelley in this poem.

The Cloud

I BRING fresh showers for the thirsting flowers,
    From the seas and the streams;
I bear light shade for the leaves when laid
    In their noon-day dreams.
From my wings are shaken the dews that waken
    The sweet buds every one,
When rocked to rest on their mother's breast,
    As she dances about the sun.
I wield the flail of the lashing hail,
    And whiten the green plains under,
And then again I dissolve it in rain,
    And laugh as I pass in thunder.

I sift the snow on the mountains below,
    And their great pines groan aghast;
And all the night 'tis my pillow white,
    While I sleep in the arms of the blast.
Sublime on the towers of my skiey bowers,
    Lightning my pilot sits;
In a cavern under is fettered the thunder,
    It struggles and howls at fits;

Over earth and ocean, with gentle motion,
    This pilot is guiding me,
Lured by the love of the genii that move
    In the depths of the purple sea;
Over the rills, and the crags, and the hills,
    Over the lakes and the plains,
Wherever he dream, under mountain or stream,
    The Spirit he loves remains;
And I all the while bask in heaven's blue smile,
    Whilst he is dissolving in rains.

The sanguine sunrise, with his meteor eyes,
   And his burning plumes outspread,
Leaps on the back of my sailing rack,
   When the morning star shines dead.
As on the jag of a mountain crag,
   Which an earthquake rocks and swings,
An eagle alit one moment may sit
   In the light of its golden wings.
And when sunset may breathe, from the lit sea beneath,
   Its ardours of rest and of love,
And the crimson pall of eve may fall
   From the depth of heaven above,
With wings folded I rest, on mine airy nest,
   As still as a brooding dove.

That orbed maiden with white fire laden,
   Whom mortals call the moon,
Glides glimmering o'er my fleece-like floor,
   By the midnight breezes strewn;
And wherever the beat of her unseen feet,
   Which only the angels hear,
May have broken the woof of my tent's thin roof,
   The stars peep behind her and peer;
And I laugh to see them whirl and flee,
   Like a swarm of golden bees,
When I widen the rent in my wind-built tent,
   Till the calm rivers, lakes, and seas,
Like strips of the sky fallen through me on high,
   Are each paved with the moon and these.

I bind the sun's throne with a burning zone,
  And the moon's with a girdle of pearl;
The volcanos are dim, and the stars reel and swim,
  When the whirlwinds my banner unfurl.
From cape to cape, with a bridge-like shape,
  Over a torrent sea,
Sunbeam-proof, I hang like a roof,
  The mountains its columns be.
The triumphal arch through which I march
  With hurricane, fire, and snow,
When the powers of the air are chained to my chair,
  Is the million-coloured bow;
The sphere-fire above its soft colours wove,
  While the moist earth was laughing below.

I am the daughter of earth and water,
  And the nursling of the sky;
I pass through the pores of the ocean and shores;
  I change, but I cannot die.
For after the rain when with never a stain,
  The pavilion of heaven is bare,
And the winds and sunbeams with their convex gleams,
  Build up the blue dome of air,
I silently laugh at my own cenotaph,
  And out of the caverns of rain,
Like a child from the womb, like a ghost from the tomb,
  I arise and unbuild it again.

'This poem was conceived and chiefly written in a wood that skirts the Arno, near Florence,' wrote Shelley, 'and on a day when the tempestuous wind, whose temperament is at once mild and animated, was collecting vapours which pour down the autumn rains'. This is considered the masterpiece of his shorter poems. There is a plaque on a modern block of flats near the station recording the site of the wood. The Shelleys had come to Florence in October, 1819, for the birth of their son Percy Florence.

Ode to the West Wind

O, WILD West Wind, thou breath of Autumn's being,
Thou, from whose unseen presence the leaves dead
Are driven, like ghosts from an enchanter fleeing,

Yellow, and black, and pale, and hectic red,
Pestilence-stricken multitudes: O, thou,
Who chariotest to their dark wintry bed

The winged seeds, where they lie cold and low,
Each like a corpse within its grave, until
Thine azure sister of the spring shall blow

Her clarion o'er the dreaming earth, and fill
(Driving sweet buds like flocks to feed in air)
With living hues and odours plain and hill:

Wild Spirit, which art moving every where;
Destroyer and preserver; hear, O, hear!

Thou on whose stream, 'mid the steep sky's commotion,
Loose clouds like earth's decaying leaves are shed,
Shook from the tangled boughs of Heaven and Ocean,

Angels of rain and lightning: there are spread
On the blue surface of thine airy surge,
Like the bright hair uplifted from the head

Of some fierce Mænad, even from the dim verge
Of the horizon to the zenith's height
The locks of the approaching storm. Thou dirge

Of the dying year, to which this closing night
Will be the dome of a vast sepulchre,
Vaulted with all thy congregated might

Of vapours, from whose solid atmosphere
Black rain and fire, and hail will burst: O, hear!

Thou who didst waken from his summer dreams
The blue Mediterranean, where he lay,
Lulled by the coil of his crystalline streams,

Beside a pumice isle in Baiæ's bay,
And saw in sleep old palaces and towers
Quivering within the wave's intenser day,

All overgrown with azure moss and flowers
So sweet, the sense faints picturing them! Thou
For whose path the Atlantic's level powers

Cleave themselves into chasms, while far below
The sea-blooms and the oozy woods which wear
The sapless foliage of the ocean, know

Thy voice, and suddenly grow grey with fear,
And tremble and despoil themselves: O, hear!

If I were a dead leaf thou mightest bear;
If I were a swift cloud to fly with thee;
A wave to pant beneath thy power, and share

The impulse of thy strength, only less free
Than thou, O, uncontroulable! If even
I were as in my boyhood, and could be

The comrade of thy wanderings over heaven,
As then, when to outstrip thy skiey speed
Scarce seemed a vision; I would ne'er have striven

As thus with thee in prayer in my sore need.
Oh! lift me as a wave, a leaf, a cloud!
I fall upon the thorns of life! I bleed!

A heavy weight of hours has chained and bowed
One too like thee: tameless, and swift, and proud.

Make me thy lyre, even as the forest is:
What if my leaves are falling like its own!
The tumult of thy mighty harmonies

Will take from both a deep, autumnal tone,
Sweet though in sadness. Be thou, spirit fierce,
My spirit! Be thou me, impetuous one!

Drive my dead thoughts over the universe
Like withered leaves to quicken a new birth!
And, by the incantation of this verse,

Scatter, as from an unextinguished hearth
Ashes and sparks, my words among mankind!
Be through my lips to unawakened earth

The trumpet of a prophecy! O, Wind,
If Winter comes, can Spring be far behind?

The death of their three-year-old son in Rome was a tragedy for the Shelleys from which they were very slow to recover. 'The hopes of my life are bound up with him,'' wrote Mary on June 5, 1819, when they were spending sleepless days and nights watching over him. Two days later William died and was buried in the cemetery at Rome. Their younger child, Clara, had died the previous year. Mary gave birth to her last child Percy Florence, in November 1819 and he lived until 1889.

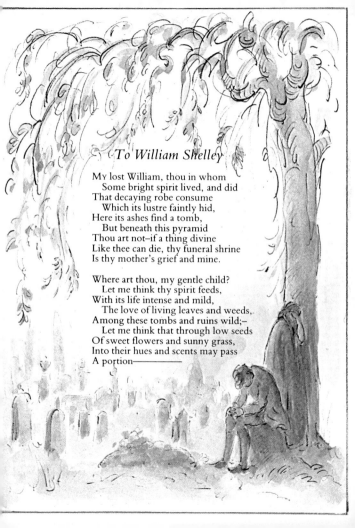

To William Shelley

My lost William, thou in whom
    Some bright spirit lived, and did
That decaying robe consume
    Which its lustre faintly hid,
Here its ashes find a tomb,
    But beneath this pyramid
Thou art not—if a thing divine
Like thee can die, thy funeral shrine
Is thy mother's grief and mine.

Where art thou, my gentle child?
    Let me think thy spirit feeds,
With its life intense and mild,
    The love of living leaves and weeds,
Among these tombs and ruins wild;—
    Let me think that through low seeds
Of sweet flowers and sunny grass,
Into their hues and scents may pass
A portion——

When the Shelleys moved back to Pisa in the Autumn of 1820 they befriended the beautiful and talented daughter of the Governor of Pisa, Teresa Viviani, who was imprisoned in a convent awaiting a marriage to be arranged by her father. This horrified the Shelleys whose ideas on freedom were so in advance of the times, and she was the inspiration for Shelley's poem 'Epipsychidion' and, it is believed, for these lyrics.

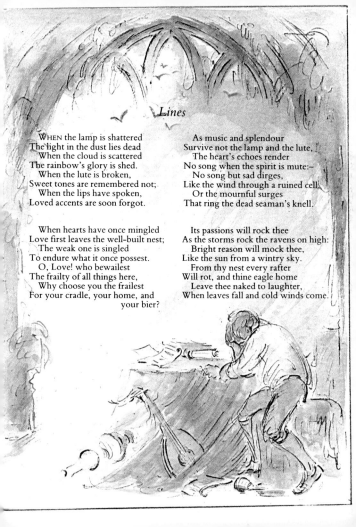

Lines

WHEN the lamp is shattered
The light in the dust lies dead
When the cloud is scattered
The rainbow's glory is shed.
 When the lute is broken,
Sweet tones are remembered not;
 When the lips have spoken,
Loved accents are soon forgot.

When hearts have once mingled
Love first leaves the well-built nest;
 The weak one is singled
To endure what it once possest.
 O, Love! who bewailest
The frailty of all things here,
 Why choose you the frailest
For your cradle, your home, and
                 your bier?

As music and splendour
Survive not the lamp and the lute,
 The heart's echoes render
No song when the spirit is mute:—
 No song but sad dirges,
Like the wind through a ruined cell,
 Or the mournful surges
That ring the dead seaman's knell.

Its passions will rock thee
As the storms rock the ravens on high:
 Bright reason will mock thee,
Like the sun from a wintry sky.
 From thy nest every rafter
Will rot, and thine eagle home
 Leave thee naked to laughter,
When leaves fall and cold winds come.

MUSIC, when soft voices die,
Vibrates in the memory—
Odours, when sweet violets sicken,
Live within the sense they quicken.
Rose leaves, when the rose is dead,
Are heaped for the beloved's bed;
And so thy thoughts, when thou art gone,
Love itself shall slumber on.

ONE word is too often profaned
    For me to profane it,
One feeling too falsely disdained
    For thee to disdain it.
One hope is too like despair
    For prudence to smother,
And pity from thee more dear
    Than that from another.

I can give not what men call love,
    But wilt thou accept not
The worship the heart lifts above
    And the Heavens reject not,
The desire of the moth for the star,
    Of the night for the morrow,
The devotion to something afar
    From the sphere of our sorrow?

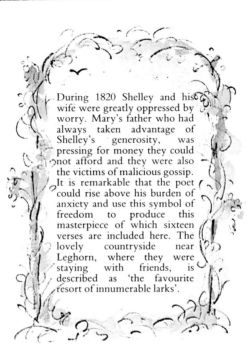

During 1820 Shelley and his wife were greatly oppressed by worry. Mary's father who had always taken advantage of Shelley's generosity, was pressing for money they could not afford and they were also the victims of malicious gossip. It is remarkable that the poet could rise above his burden of anxiety and use this symbol of freedom to produce this masterpiece of which sixteen verses are included here. The lovely countryside near Leghorn, where they were staying with friends, is described as 'the favourite resort of innumerable larks'.

To a Skylark

Hail to thee, blithe spirit!
  Bird thou never wert,
That from heaven, or near it,
  Pourest thy full heart
In profuse strains of unpremeditated art.

Higher still and higher
  From the earth thou springest
Like a cloud of fire;
  The blue deep thou wingest,
And singing still dost soar, and soaring ever singest.

In the golden lightning
  Of the sunken sun,
O'er which clouds are brightning,
  Thou dost float and run;
Like an unbodied joy whose race is just begun.

The pale purple even
  Melts around thy flight;
Like a star of heaven,
  In the broad day-light
Thou art unseen, but yet I hear thy shrill delight,

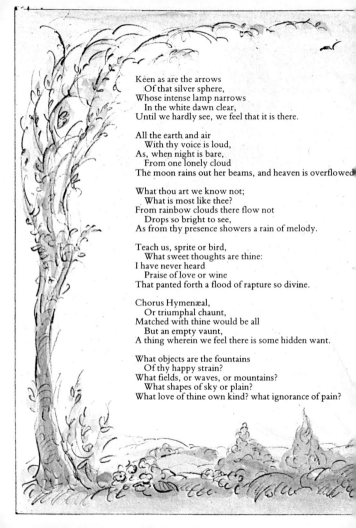

Keen as are the arrows
   Of that silver sphere,
Whose intense lamp narrows
   In the white dawn clear,
Until we hardly see, we feel that it is there.

All the earth and air
   With thy voice is loud,
As, when night is bare,
   From one lonely cloud
The moon rains out her beams, and heaven is overflowed.

What thou art we know not;
   What is most like thee?
From rainbow clouds there flow not
   Drops so bright to see,
As from thy presence showers a rain of melody.

Teach us, sprite or bird,
   What sweet thoughts are thine:
I have never heard
   Praise of love or wine
That panted forth a flood of rapture so divine.

Chorus Hymenæal,
   Or triumphal chaunt,
Matched with thine would be all
   But an empty vaunt,
A thing wherein we feel there is some hidden want.

What objects are the fountains
   Of thy happy strain?
What fields, or waves, or mountains?
   What shapes of sky or plain?
What love of thine own kind? what ignorance of pain?

With thy clear keen joyance
    Languor cannot be:
Shadow of annoyance
    Never came near thee:
Thou lovest; but ne'er knew love's sad satiety.

Waking or asleep,
    Thou of death must deem
Things more true and deep
    Than we mortals dream,
Or how could thy notes flow in such a crystal stream?

We look before and after,
    And pine for what is not:
Our sincerest laughter
    With some pain is fraught;
Our sweetest songs are those that tell of saddest thought.

Yet if we could scorn
    Hate, and pride, and fear;
If we were things born
    Not to shed a tear,
I know not how thy joy we ever should come near.

Better than all measures
    Of delightful sound,
Better than all treasures
    That in books are found,
Thy skill to poet were, thou scorner of the ground!

Teach me half the gladness
    That thy brain must know,
Such harmonious madness
    From my lips would flow,
The world should listen then, as I am listening now.

Throughout his life Shelley was deeply affected by music and easily enchanted by the musical performances of his women friends. Mary's step-sister, Claire, who lived with the Shelleys, had, according to her instructor, 'a voice like a string of pearls' and Jane Williams, wife of the friend who drowned with Shelley magnetized him with her guitar playing. Both women were the inspiration of some of his best poems.

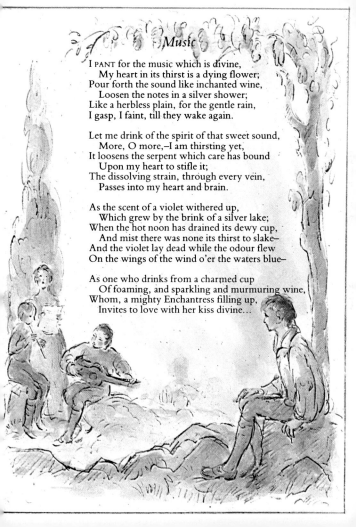

Music

I PANT for the music which is divine,
 My heart in its thirst is a dying flower;
Pour forth the sound like inchanted wine,
 Loosen the notes in a silver shower;
Like a herbless plain, for the gentle rain,
I gasp, I faint, till they wake again.

Let me drink of the spirit of that sweet sound,
 More, O more,—I am thirsting yet,
It loosens the serpent which care has bound
 Upon my heart to stifle it;
The dissolving strain, through every vein,
 Passes into my heart and brain.

As the scent of a violet withered up,
 Which grew by the brink of a silver lake;
When the hot noon has drained its dewy cup,
 And mist there was none its thirst to slake—
And the violet lay dead while the odour flew
On the wings of the wind o'er the waters blue—

As one who drinks from a charmed cup
 Of foaming, and sparkling and murmuring wine,
Whom, a mighty Enchantress filling up,
 Invites to love with her kiss divine...

This poem was published in *The Examiner* in 1818. Its editor, Leigh Hunt, whose radical opinions led him into difficulties and a prison sentence, recognized the genuis of both Shelley and Keats long before anyone else. Leigh Hunt and his large family relied on the unfailing generosity of Shelley who finally arranged for them to come and live in Italy. A few days after settling them in Pisa (where Byron had been persuaded to loan them part of his Palazzo Lanfranchi) Shelley met his death by drowning on his way home from Leghorn to San Terenzo when his boat capsized in a storm.

Ozymandias

I MET a traveller from an antique land
Who said: Two vast and trunkless legs of stone
Stand in the desert. Near them, on the sand,
Half sunk, a shattered visage lies, whose frown,
And wrinkled lip, and sneer of cold command,
Tell that its sculptor well those passions read
Which yet survive, stamped on these lifeless things,
The hand that mocked them, and the heart that fed:
And on the pedestal these words appear:
'My name is Ozymandias, king of kings:
Look on my works, ye Mighty, and despair!'
Nothing beside remains. Round the decay
Of that colossal wreck, boundless and bare
The lone and level sands stretch far away.

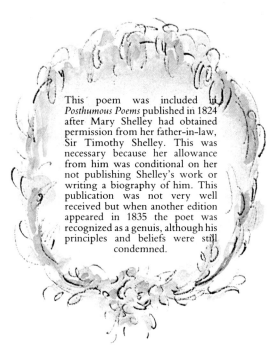

This poem was included in *Posthumous Poems* published in 1824 after Mary Shelley had obtained permission from her father-in-law, Sir Timothy Shelley. This was necessary because her allowance from him was conditional on her not publishing Shelley's work or writing a biography of him. This publication was not very well received but when another edition appeared in 1835 the poet was recognized as a genuis, although his principles and beliefs were still condemned.

A Bridal Song

THE golden gates of Sleep unbar
    Where Strength and Beauty met together,
Kindle their image like a star
    In a sea of glassy weather.
Night, with all thy stars look down,–
    Darkness, weep thy holiest dew,–
Never smiled the inconstant moon
    On a pair so true.
Let eyes not see their own delight;–
Haste swift Hour, and thy flight
    Oft renew.

Fairies, sprites, and angels keep her!
    Holy stars, permit no wrong!
And return to wake the sleeper,
    Dawn,–ere it be long!
Oh joy! oh fear! what will be done
In the absence of the sun!
    Come along!

The legend of Proserpine (Persephone) Goddess of Vegetation, abducted by Pluto and forced to live in the Underworld, is an exciting one. She was the daughter of Demeter (or Ceres) Goddess of Agriculture, and when she was not assisting her mother she would hasten to Sicily, her favourite resort. It was while she and her following of nymphs were gathering flowers on the slopes of Mount Aetna that she was first seen by Pluto, driving past in his dark chariot drawn by four fiery coal-black steeds.

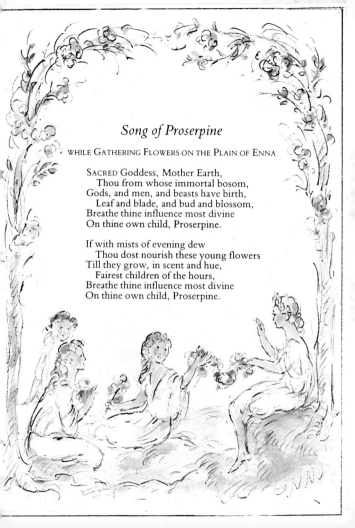

Song of Proserpine

SACRED Goddess, Mother Earth,
  Thou from whose immortal bosom,
Gods, and men, and beasts have birth,
  Leaf and blade, and bud and blossom,
Breathe thine influence most divine
On thine own child, Proserpine.

If with mists of evening dew
  Thou dost nourish these young flowers
Till they grow, in scent and hue,
  Fairest children of the hours,
Breathe thine influence most divine
On thine own child, Proserpine.